EADAR

charles yerkes

EADAR

uncommon land, uncommon lives

TATE PUBLISHING & *Enterprises*

Eadar
Copyright © 2009 by Charles Yerkes. All rights reserved.

No part of this publication may be reproduced, stored in a retrieval system or transmitted in any way by any means, electronic, mechanical, photocopy, recording or otherwise without the prior permission of the author except as provided by USA copyright law.

The opinions expressed by the author are not necessarily those of Tate Publishing, LLC.

Published by Tate Publishing & Enterprises, LLC
127 E. Trade Center Terrace | Mustang, Oklahoma 73064 USA
1.888.361.9473 | www.tatepublishing.com

Tate Publishing is committed to excellence in the publishing industry. The company reflects the philosophy established by the founders, based on Psalm 68:11,
"The Lord gave the word and great was the company of those who published it."

Book design copyright © 2009 by Tate Publishing, LLC. All rights reserved.
Cover design by Lance Waldrop
Interior design by Stefanie Rooney

Published in the United States of America

ISBN: 978-1-61566-501-3
1. Fiction, Folklore
10.03.03

DEDICATION

This book is dedicated to my mom and dad who always supported me, no matter the direction my adventurous life has led. Without their support this book would never have been possible. Thank you.

CONTENTS

9	Eadar
15	Black Molly
21	Keala Pursuing Rest
25	Old Tom Barley
31	Allon
39	The Fishing Trip
45	A Beautiful Day?
47	Tristan
55	A Chance Meeting
63	Alone on a Hill
65	Yet Again
69	The Rescue
95	Corbin and the Widow Mimms
105	Patience
111	The Rite
117	Different Drummer
125	Out of the Storm

EADAR

I will tell you of a land whose high king made it possible for it to become a divided country, often bitterly so. Now worry not, this will not be a sad tale, nor is it a complete history. Those can be the makings of a rather boring story. No, this will only be an introductory account, one that will help lend some sense to all other stories of the Eadar. It is a land of but one king, yet, of many allegiances. Treacherous sounding, is it not? Yes, it is a country full of traitors, but one even fuller of patriots, the ones whose loyalty to the king runs deep and true. Oh, where to begin? Why not at the beginning?

Yes, we will start at the beginning with the king, with the great high king. His name is Iarna—Iarna the Good, the Just, the Bold and Daring Risk Taker, the Unpredictable, and it is Jubal the Joyous. All these names and many more. It is the name *The Bold and Daring Risk Taker* that interests us now. For it is by a risk he took that the possibility of division first entered Eadar.

I know what you are thinking: *A good king should not be taking unnecessary risks with his people.* He couldn't agree with you more. That would be careless, thoughtless, and negligent. Those are not the risks he takes. His are always thought out, weighed carefully, and planned well. But there comes a time when thinking produces no more solutions, when there is nothing left to weigh, and when things that are to happen can only happen outside the framework of carefully laid plans. It is then, at that moment, that moving forward and taking the risk becomes bold and daring. If the risk pays off, he is the hero; if not … he is overthrown.

So, what was this risk? It had to do with the founding of Eadar. I guess you could say that his risk taking was first evident at the country's inception. For it was founded on his dream of being more to his people than just their high king. Now you may be thinking, *That doesn't sound strange.* But wait until you hear what he meant by "being more." He did not want more power or a more elevated position. No, he simply wanted more than their admiration. He wanted his people's love. Ah, to be loved. What person doesn't want that? To have friends, companions… the problem was, he was still king. Any friends he would make must be able to accommodate his royalty and authority, no questions asked. Between you and me, it would have been easier if he had simply wanted more power. Here is another complication; in order to gain a friend, you must give up control. Once you have relinquished control, anything can happen and it usually does.

To give up control and still remain king, the intricacies of this could prove to be a royal pain. His answer was the establishment of the clans, allowing the people to govern themselves, under his influence, under his direction, but not under control. He risked the gaining of more than mere admiration, the gaining of friends and comrades … of love, against losing everything. Quite the bold and daring risk, is it not?

Has it been worth it, you ask? Well, it has not gone as well as he would have liked. In fact, it has caused him the greatest of all pain, but it has not gone as unsuccessfully as it may have either. Indeed, Iarna has oft been heard saying, "The dream lives on!" So he definitely thinks it has been worth it, and he has acquired many friends.

True, there are noble lords who make alliances with and concessions to the great enemy Brokine (the enemy who hates forever). Doing so, as they say, "Out of allegiance to the crown." But there are also those who, upon hearing a lord so speak, either quickly agree with that lord, saying that he did so out of allegiance to the crown, since the crown is a measure of money in Eadar. Or they agree by saying, "Sure enough now, he is out of allegiance with the king." And it is noteworthy that the wealth of these ruling lords often increases drastically when they make these alliances.

But that is Eadar, the land of risk. One whose clans often war with each other, whose leaders make alliances with the great enemy, and yet it is a country that knows great peace and joy; for many are they who are now friends of the king, whose loyalty to the king remains alive and strong. It is a land where pain, tears, excitement, and joy are found happening all at the same time, a very complicated place.

I don't know what else to say that would not make this much too long of an introduction. Many are the tales from Eadar. You will learn more about this land with each new telling. Until next time, my friends, dream well.

BLACK MOLLY

Molly Luane was her given name, and she ran the local inn, owned it really. It was one of the finest inns in all the lands of the Eadar, not one of the biggest, but certainly one of the best. She worked very hard to keep it that way. To do this meant that every now and then she had to lend a hand to help things run smoothly. She would do this whenever help was needed no matter the reason. Be it someone not showing up for work or their suddenly becoming very busy, with more work than the scheduled help could handle. Whether it was cooking, cleaning, or serving the tables their food, she would do whatever it took to keep her customers happy and coming back. That was of utmost importance.

The night she received the name Black Molly was one of the busiest she had ever seen, and Molly was helping serve the tables. This was also the night of the most severe rainstorm in living memory. It was raining so hard that you could not see your hand at arm's length. It was a night on which everyone was seeking some sort of shelter, be that home or the inn, with most choosing Molly's inn, for the hospitality and cooking at Molly's was the stuff from which legends are made.

Among the guests that night were two whose intentions, how can I say this gently, were slightly less than honorable. These two came with the purpose of having some amusement with Molly, at her expense. This is what happened.

The unsuspecting Molly came to their table, took their order, and then turned to go. At which point, one of the men reached out and grabbed

Molly around the waist and pulled her close, and said, "Come here my pretty lady."

Oh, you've never seen a man lose two teeth so rapidly as did he. Typically, Molly was a compassionate woman, known to be kind and giving to a fault. But she was also known to not be overly warm to indecencies. She spun around so swiftly and slapped him so solidly that, as I said, he lost two teeth, and the whole room went silent as everyone turned to see what had just happened, for no one had ever heard it thunder inside the inn before.

The man who just lost his teeth sat in stunned silence, not comprehending what had just happened. But his companion, who, being more quick witted and in slightly less pain, said, "That was a cold and black-hearted thing to do, Molly. He meant no harm; he was just having a bit of fun."

"With fun such as yours," said Molly, "you should be grateful that this cold, black heart isn't also full of ice. Now since my company is too cold and black for you, perhaps you'll be leaving, preferring to be out in the rain."

"Well, no, Molly. I didn't mean—"

"Go, I said, the both of you." As she said this, all the other men in the room rose, prepared to come to Molly's aid if need be.

"Go," she said, "before I have you thrown out."

Slowly the two looked around the room, stood, and made their way out into the pouring rain. Molly turned to the man standing beside her and said, "Tom, please see to it that they do no mischief on their way out."

"Certainly," he said, "anything for you, oh Black-hearted Molly."

For which he barely got out of the door without getting slapped himself, which brought an eruption of laughter from everyone in the room. From that point on, everyone, much to Molly's dismay began calling for Black-hearted Molly. It was, "Black-hearted Molly, more food please. Oh Black-hearted Molly, I need something more to drink." Black-hearted Molly this, Black-hearted Molly that, everywhere she turned, she was called Black-hearted Molly. For the rest of the night, this is how things went. Well, I say the rest of the night, but as the evening progressed, her patrons found Black-hearted Molly just much too much to say. So they simply started calling for Black Molly. Molly did not find this to be much of an improvement. To make matters worse, by noon the next day, the whole town had heard about her knocking that man's teeth out. The whole town was then calling her Black Molly.

Molly hoped that after a day or two, this would all pass, that it would all settle down and everyone would once again simply call her Molly. But no, the town was as settled as it would get. To this day, she is still called Black Molly. Though, in truth, she sort of liked this new name. It had a ring to it, *Black Molly;* mysterious and intriguing it was. Oh, the fun she could have with such a name. If only there was someone left in town who didn't know the rather undignified way in which she earned it. Poor Molly.

That is the story of how Black Molly got her name.

KEALA
PURSUING REST

Keala walks out of the mist and crosses a brown wet land. In the spring this would all be green—the grass, the trees. But now it was only bleak brown and barren with the sky looking very much like it would snow.

Despite herself, Keala loved the cold. Rather, she loved how she felt as she warmed up from being cold. One of her favorite memories of home is the relaxed sleepy feeling she would get whenever she would come in from the cold and start to warm up, all bundled in a thick quilt while sipping some warm soup. What she wouldn't give now for just one cup of her mother's vegetable soup.

These were her thoughts as her eyes danced across the landscape that stretched out before her. There was something about this land, something peaceful, something quiet, as if the land itself were asleep. As she is pondering this, a white blanket begins to fall from the sky, coming down one white flake at a time.

According to the information she had been given, there was a house nearby where she could stay—nothing fancy, but a warm house that would be dry. With one last look around, she starts to move, for she only enjoys being out in the cold and watching the snow fall; whenever she can get inside quickly to warm up. But as it is, she is tired, very, very tired, and she does not know how much further she has yet to travel. But, she should be close. She hopes she is close; there are not many hours of daylight left. And she knows the dangers of being outside on a cold winter's night. Never mind being caught in a snowstorm while exhausted.

She climbs to the top of one more hill, and there it is, sitting just inside the tree line on the other side of the clearing. A smile crosses her face. Her journey is almost over; soon she will be seated in a warm room, eating a hot meal, and who knows, she might even find an extra quilt to wrap herself in. She hurries across the clearing.

Rest well, little cousin; rest well.

OLD TOM BARLEY

Old Tom Barley is finally coming home, traveling once again the old familiar roads. Around every bend he finds a memory, yet he has no time to slow down and reminisce if he is to make his destination on time. For too long now he has promised himself that if ever he were close enough, he would once again watch the sun set over his old hometown of Elberon. It is one of his favorite memories from so long ago—sitting on his majestic throne of power while watching the sunset as the wind caused wave upon wave of grass to flow past him.

Throne of power... laughs he to himself while hurrying on. Yet, even pushing on with all due haste, it is late in the day when he finally arrives at the base of the hill. His pulse quickens for he is very near his destination and he still has a chance to be on time. At the top of this hill sits the throne. Quickly he begins to climb.

This throne, which sat atop the tallest of the hills overlooking Elberon, was only an outcropping of rock, one that time, wind, and rain had fashioned into a natural seat. Yet it was from here he had ruled great kingdoms. Ruled kingdoms, dispensed justice, slew dragons, and saved many a beautiful princess. Oh the simplicities of childhood play; these are the memories freshest in this mind. He moves forward as quickly as possible.

About halfway up, an unwanted thought crosses his mind. *What if the throne is not there? There is no accounting for what could have happened over the years. Is this to be yet another disappointment and my journey home for naught?* He is worrying over this as he draws close to the top of the hill and does not see the throne. His pace actually slows for fear that it is gone. Yet the sun will not wait; he presses on. An eternity seems to pass as he approaches the crest of the hill. *Will it be there? Will it...* He pauses and stills himself against the possibility that it might not. He climbs to the top of the hill, and there it is, just past the hill's crest, his majestic throne of power, just as he has left it. He runs the last few steps to this prized destination.

Now that he is here, he pauses, almost unable to believe he has actually made it. Reverently he sits down, and as he does so, he is overcome with a mixture of emotion, feeling very foolish and very exhilarated; foolish because he had worried about an outcropping of rock, and overjoyed because he would now be able to watch the sun set while sitting upon his old throne. Once seated, he begins to survey the surrounding countryside, marveling at the beauty in what he sees with his eyes soon coming to rest upon Elberon, the little town far below. It's a small place, yet one filled with the hustle and bustle of very important people, doing...well...very important things. With all he has seen, he hopes for their sake that they will be able to dream forever so.

His gaze then wanders across the slopes of the surrounding hills. It has been a long time since he's lived here and longer still since being carefree, as when last he sat here. As he is pondering these things, a breeze begins to blow, sending wave upon wave of tall grass cascading over the hillside. He becomes speechless as tears of joy come to his eyes, for the moment he has long anticipated finally arrives: the setting of the sun over Elberon. It is one of the few times in his life when his expectations are exceeded: the grass flowing, the fragrances of holly and honeysuckle pungent in the air, and the setting sun bathing the land in its golden hue. As the sun kisses the rooftops of Elberon, that mundane little town is once again transformed into his town of enchantment from so long ago. Then, as it slowly passes out of sight, the sun paints the sky. A masterful artist who used ever shifting tones, he first added yellow to the evening sky, then he added more tones, changing yellow to amber, amber to orange, orange to an amazingly beautiful red, and then transforming this red into a brilliant magenta before allowing the colors to fade through gray and settle into the blackness of night.

It has been a good day. He had to travel fast and furiously, but arriving in time to watch this has made it all worthwhile. He remains seated for quite some time not wanting this moment to end; then standing he makes ready to leave, for there can be no great rest here for one such as he, a man no longer welcome in his own hometown. Another memory now comes to mind, one that brings a different sort of tear. But no, he will not ruin this moment by remembering that which he cannot change.

Oh, it is so good to be here again. Even if the stay is brief and no one knows I ever came, he thinks. As he looks out over his mountain sanctuary one last time, a place now bathed in the light of the moon. Then he inhales deeply, savoring the sweet night air. He is so grateful that his childhood throne is still here. Somehow, it just wouldn't have been the same without it. He then turns and fades into the night. Farther down the road, he will find rest at a place where he is most welcome. But for now, he must take joy where and as he can and the joy he has found this evening will speak to him for a very long time … a very long time.

ALLON

There was once a man injured and alone resting by the side of the road, gathering some strength that he might travel a little farther toward home before the fall of night. His name was Allon. As he sat there, he thought back over all that had recently befallen. His mind went back to a morning, a morning now so long ago, the morning when he had ridden forth with the great host, banners flying, trumpets blaring, armor glistening in the morning sun—an impressive sight to behold. He then remembered the fighting, it had been his best ever, at least until he had become severely wounded. Then he remembered the source of his greatest pain. A pain, which came not from his wounds, nor could he blame his mortal enemies, the Eadarians, for this pain. The source of this bitter pain was the very one for whom he had fought.

He served the dark lord Brokine. Whose words about the fallen, those such as he, who were too weak, too injured to fight on, came back to his mind now with a maddening clarity. Brokine had said, "The fallen are the fallen. They are either one less foe to fight or one less mouth to feed. What care I who falls where? If they can make it back on their own, fine. I'll use them again later. If not, just as well. I have reserves. Come! Leave them. We have other places to be." He was then abandoned, quicker than a worn out shoe, and this when he had given his all.

He was so weary that, before he realized what was happening, he had nodded off to sleep. He did not sleep long, for he was awakened quite suddenly by a very strange sound, a sound that his weary mind could not place at first. But it was a sound that he knew he should not be hearing. Not here, not now. It was... it was... whistling. Someone was whistling a tune, a very merry tune. Yet it was one he did not know. When in enemy territory, that is not such a good thing. As weak and defenseless as he was, the last thing he wanted to do was to face an enemy soldier, one who was fresh and ready to fight. Quickly he looked for a place to hide, but alas, there was none. In truth, even if there had been, he was too weak to move let alone hide. He gritted his teeth, for come what may he had to face it. Thankfully, what came into view was not a fresh enemy soldier, but rather a man very much like himself, a man whose origins he could not identify, but one who was as injured as he was. One who also walked with shoulders stooped in the weariness of wounds but freshly bound. Allon's fear gave way to amazement. Amazement that such a joyous tune could come out of such a weary traveler. He was even more amazed when this stranger drew near and stopped whistling. For even though the man before him was barely able to stand, there was still an incredible strength and power to be seen in him—strength that, as he looked the stranger in the eyes, he knew to be different from the mere brutish force possessed by his lord. It was a strength he found inspiring and intimidating, calming and disquieting, certain and unpredictable. Quiet, steady, and running very deep, it was a strength that Allon had never seen.

The man stopped in front of Allon and asked if he could join him in the shade, the only shade for miles. "You may," said Allon. But not yet trusting this new companion, he continued, "But stay over there, where I can keep an eye on you."

"As you wish," came the reply.

The stranger sat down. Allon watched him closely, marveling at the quiet power that he perceived in the man. Soon curiosity overcame mistrust, and Allon decided to speak to his new companion. He said, "My name is Allon. I am from Undreemor."

"My name is Jon. I am from Eadar," came the reply.

Anger and indignation quickly arose in Allon,

pushing all thought of pleasant conversation aside. Here sat the enemy. "Eadarian, I might have known! I have heard that you are arrogant cowards, ones who do not respect anyone but yourselves and then seek to coerce your way of life onto those who live in neighboring lands. You are a disease that must be annihilated before it spreads." Allon wanted to fight. At least a war of words, for neither man was capable of a physical contest.

"Really?" said Jon, as he closed his eyes to rest.

Surprised but not deterred by such an unexpected response, Allon tried again. "Yes, and it is your kind who has done this to me," he said, indicating his wounded state, knowing that at the very least this should provoke the man to be defensive. When once a man is defensive, he is but a short step away form being provoked into a fight.

"So, we have something in common. It is my own people who have done this to me," said Jon.

Allon was stunned. He had assumed that Jon's wounds were received from fighting Brokine's army. It is easy to be angry with an enemy. But here was a man beaten near to death by his own people, a man who had not the manner of a coward or a criminal but that of a hero. A man he could respect. Allon's anger began to subside. He was at a loss for words. What do you say to a man whose own people have turned against him? After an extended silence, he managed to ask, "In truth?"

"In truth," said Jon.

Jon would speak no more of this, for the pain was still much too near. Allon could respect this, for he too was not ready to speak of his betrayal by Brokine. However, now that conversation had begun, and since it was Allon who had initiated it, it would be a shame to stop now. They talked of many things that day; discussing everything from military tactics, to their mothers' home cooking. So it was that a friendship began. These two men, men from warring countries, from opposing points of view, were drawn together by something bigger than either one of them—the commonality of their pain. Allon enjoyed that day more than many he could remember. As time was drawing near for them to part ways, he marveled at this. How could he enjoy this man's company so much, a man who was supposed to be his enemy? He did not know. Nor did he wish this time to end.

He said, "My way lies south and this road is not safe for one man alone. If your way also lies south, perhaps we could travel together for a while."

"Perhaps," said Jon. "Perhaps."

"Come, Eadarian, you were traveling in the same direction as I when you arrived. Why not join me now? At least until our paths do part."

Jon closed his eyes as he considered this for a moment. Then he said, "All right. Yes we will travel together, you and I. At least for a while."

"Good, Eadarian! Good," said Allon as he prepared to continue the journey, though Jon remained motionless. "Well come on, Eadarian, we have far to go."

Jon raised an eyebrow, a sighed ponderously, and wondered if he had just made a poor decision. But he also stood and made ready to leave.

These two unlikely companions then traveled together for many days, had many adventures, and became fast friends. All of which are stories for another time. Until that time, they wish a road for you to travel and a song for you to sing.

THE FISHING TRIP

For a long time, he simply stood there and watched as the morning mist rose from the lake. Then he let his eyes slowly drift to the mountains beyond, which were standing majestically against the sky. And he pondered, *Has it really been that long ago since I have been able to stand here and admire this view?*

That had been … on a rare day, a magnificent day, a day spent with his father in the pursuit of the *wild* fish. Neither man was a fisherman by trade, but they loved to go. They loved the quietness of the lake, the pitting of themselves against the wilds of nature. Nature usually won. But there were few things these men loved more. Now, one of those things was simply spending time together while doing things they both loved. But this particular day had held even more meaning for Keagan, Tom's father. Tom wished that he had then known how much more. Though perhaps, it was better that he had not. Maybe some things were better left for time to reveal.

By the time of this outing, Keagan had watched Tom grow to be a man. He was still a young man, yes, but by all reckoning, he had left boyhood behind. He was a man, a fine, fine man. Soon he would be out of his parent's house, on his own, making his own mark upon the world. His parents were very proud of him. Yet, they knew that young men such as Tom could not long live in their village. For young men such as he, who courageously asked the tough questions, who were fearless in having those questions answered, and who were then daring enough to live a life based upon the answers received, were often viewed by their nobility as problems and as threats to be eliminated instead of assets to be harnessed.

Keagan and Sara had seen this too often with the sons of others. They knew that Tom would be forced to leave. That was why this day was so special for Keagan. It might well be the last such day he could spend with his son. *Yes,* thought Tom, *some things are better left for time to reveal.*

They had arrived early and fished hard all morning, fishing the shallows, along the banks, under the shadiest trees, around the brush piles, everywhere that the *wild* fish liked to be. And by mid-afternoon they had caught an ample supply of pleasant conversation. Suddenly, Tom spotted a large fish, a very large fish, lying just offshore in some shallow water. Slowly Tom moved toward it. If he could just get a little closer, they would have at least one fish this day. He moved closer, closer, closer; this fish was going to be his. It was almost in his grasp. When suddenly, from behind, there came a loud cry, and before Tom could react, he found himself lying face down in the shallows; right where his fish had been.

Even as he fell headfirst into the water, he knew what had happened. And while still under the water, he heard his father's laughter. As Tom stood up, he had one thing on his mind. It wasn't catching fish. Tom could not remember whose head went under the water most often, but he did remember being impressed by the fact that for an old man, his father held his own quite well. He also remembered that this was the first time he had ever seen the leaves of those giant oaks drip with water, without it having rained. After a particularly strenuous bout, while both men were pausing to catch their breaths, Keagan nodded toward the island at the other end of the lake and asked, "Think you can beat the old man?" With a quick smile from Tom, they were off, swimming just as fast as they could. It really did not matter who won. They were thoroughly enjoying themselves; that was enough.

By the time they reached the island shore, all their energy was spent. They climbed onto the grassy bank and stretched out. They lay there for a long time, relaxing while staring up at the sky. The day would soon be over, and neither wanted to be the first to end it. At length they sat up and stared at the distant mountains. "This has been a good day," said Keagan.

"Yes, it has," said Tom.

That was all that was said for quite some time, as each simply enjoyed the other's company. The quiet companionship of men is often more rewarding than idle conversation.

They stayed on the island as long as possible then enjoyed a calm and unhurried swim back to shore. They gathered their gear and started for home. They talked now but in hushed tones. Louder tones would have stolen the moment, tarnished the day. Life would return to its normal level as they approached home. But for now, the magic of the moment lingered as these two strong men walked side by side. They paused at the place where they had watched the sun rise. It was now early evening and the sun was setting low in the sky. The valley looked so peaceful. Keagan said, "This has been a good day. One worthy of remembrance." Tom had merely nodded in response, and then turning, the two had traveled home.

As he stood there again, after so many years, Tom said, "Yes. It is well worth remembering." Then as the sun rose high into the sky, it caused shadow patterns from the clouds to paint the countryside in shades of tone that made it seem more rich, more alive than before. While he watched this and remembered his father, Tom decided to change course and visit his mother. "For," he said quietly, "some things are not better left for time to reveal."

A BEAUTIFUL DAY?

It is a beautiful day, sunny and warm, a perfect day to be on the coast. Yet Logon finds himself wishing that a thunderous storm would blow in. Now it has been said that Logon is a little odd. Not that there is anything wrong with him; he just doesn't walk upon the well-worn paths, if you take my meaning.

While most enjoy the warmth of the sun, the smoothness of the sand, the gentle rhythm of the waves lapping against the shore, and the light touch of a midsummer's breeze, Logon loves the churning of the clouds, the taste of the salt air as the breeze intensifies into a mighty wind, the great gray of the sea moving and swelling with white caps smashing against the rocky shore.

These contain power, strength, and vibrancy, which he finds comforting as he stands upon a rocky cliff and watches the awakening of the great deep. There is something refreshing, rejuvenating about it. So much so, that as he leaves the coast, he needs silence about him for a while. Words, sounds, only serve to diminish the experience in some way. He really couldn't tell you why, but it is so.

He looks up at the clear blue sky then down upon the docile waves, which are casually rolling onto the shore. He closes his eyes, feels the breeze play across his face, and run its fingers through his hair, and then sighs deeply. It's not all he would have wished for, *But,* he thinks as he sits down to absorb the day, *it will do. Yes … it will do. There is always next time. And perhaps next time it will truly be a beautiful day.*

TRISTAN

Tristan could only stand and stare. The ruins before him had been a house at which he had anticipated a warm welcome and perhaps an even warmer meal. But now his freedom was extended even from these. Most of the house was now a pile of rubble, a rubbish heap of wood and stone with the remainder looking... not much better. And if this added freedom weren't infuriating enough, the storm that brewed on the horizon promised to add yet another freedom to his life;

that from being dry. Sometimes freedom was slightly overrated.

As you may have noticed, Tristan had been thinking about freedom lately. Okay, he had been thinking about little else, though it was mostly his "free from's" and not his freedoms that had become bothersome and even downright troubling. Out of necessity, his life had left him free from home, family, clan, kin, companionship, the predictable, and all those small things that make life, well … not so troubled.

Then staring at the wreckage before him, he remembered something he had dreamed about as a boy, the freedom of the Jarr-Dann. As a boy of no more than eight or so, he heard stories of wondrous adventurers simply known as Jarr-Dann— dashing cavaliers, near mythic adventurers who feared nothing. Bold rebels they were, whose only loyalties were to king and country, those who were unafraid to clash with errant noble lords, such as his own. Anyway, by about the age of thirteen, his passionate dream had become to live the life of a Jarr-Dann, one who roamed the world free! Free from worry. Free from fear. Free from restraint. "And free from good dinners and safe dry places to sleep," he added, being freed from this memory as the first raindrops spattered into his face.

Well, there was no hope for it now but to seek some shelter. He turned his steps toward the ruins, this place of lost welcome, to see what might be had. As he began his search, words unbidden came pouring through his mind. Words he had not heard in years but remembered now so clearly, so audibly, he could actually hear the tone in Jon's voice as he spoke them, "No mother wants her child to have to live as I do. Yet no mother wants her child not to be able to, if at some point he must."

"Well, Jon," Tristan said with a sigh, "it seems as if now I'm at the point of must."

Fortunately he found that part of the house could still offer shelter from the rain. True, what was left was little more than a lean-to, yet as long as the wind didn't shift he would be able to stay dry. If this were more of a shelter he would have made a fire. Yet, as it was, it would not have been safe to do so, for if the wind changed direction he might burn down what shelter he had. Though it was tempting, for a fire's warmth would have added a small level of comfort and all levels of that were now severely missing. Just then the wind did shift and sprayed him with rain. "But this is not more of a shelter," he admitted as he moved what little distance he could from the lean-to's edge. Then with nothing else to do, he began to watch the rain.

To think he had once wanted to live this life, well to be a Jarr-Dann anyway. He hadn't really known all that would include. His mother had and she knew it was short sighted to seek it out. But young enterprising boys tend not to listen to those who matter most. So she had arranged for Jon Minor, a great leader among the Jarr-Dann, to meet with Tristan and give him the truth about life as a Jarr-Dann. To tell him all those little things that never made it into the exciting stories of which he was so fond. Little things such as: a sever lack of comfortable lodgings, hunger from a persistent lack of food, of being cold, wet, and miserable due to consistent lack of shelter, and of being isolated from family and friends, just to name a few minor omissions.

Just then lightning flashed, thunder roared, and a drop of rain found its way through the roof of his shelter and onto the back of his neck. Tristan looked up at the roof and added to that list, as he thought aloud, "Of having to scrounge for shelter from the pouring rain." He moved to avoid the next drop.

He remembered being so excited at being able to meet one of his heroes, for, without trying, Jon had gained a reputation that was legendary as a leader among those dashing cavaliers. There were so many questions he had wanted to ask. The meeting had been very short, and Tristan could not remember everything that was said. But he did remember being shocked at Jon not wanting him to become a Jarr-Dann. "Why do you want to join us who are so marked?" he asked.

"Out of loyalty to the king," came Tristan's quick reply.

"Not all who are loyal are forced to live as we do. Indeed, some live quite comfortably and well. Why not choose to live as they?"

"But there is no adventure there!"

"Ah, the real reason."

Jon then began to tell Tristan about the long lonely hours spent crossing the rain swept moors, of having been forced to travel far on a cold winter's night with no shelter to be found along the way, of being suspected and despised by men when he had done nothing wrong, and of rarely meeting any other Jarr-Dann. The life of a Jarr-Dann was for the most part a lonely life. For, "We are not a clan but the cast outs of many. We have no place to meet and gather. Do not confuse a forced isolation for roaming free."

Tristan fired back, "You're just saying this because my mother wants you to! She put you up to this just to make me behave and choose the life she wants for me."

"No. No mother wants her child to have to live as I do. Yet, no mother wants her child not to be able to if at some point he must. She does not want to force you to be anything. That would only cripple your ability to be a strong man and pursue loyalty to the king. She knows that your desire is not about loyalty but only adventure, excitement, and daring deeds. These are never good reasons to choose anything."

"Why did you choose to become one then?" asked Tristan.

"Why did I…" Jon paused before continuing. "I did not choose. It was imposed upon me. I was only ever loyal to our king. I lived a quiet life and enjoyed it very much; sometimes I still dream about it. But I voiced opposition over the earl's treatment of the poor. This opposition gained more and more support, and the earl felt the only way to stop it was to banish me. Banish me 'for the sake of the king.'"

"So, he made you a Jarr-Dann?"

"Yes, I was banished for loyalty to the king. And there has been more than one day when that loyalty, the love of and for my king, has been the only thing that has kept me moving. So you see, Tristan, in the truest sense, you cannot choose to be a Jarr-Dann. It is only when you are forced down that path for being true to the king that you will have the strength to endure it.

"As I said earlier," Jon continued, "your mother sees that you are a strong boy, and she wants you to become an even stronger man. She knows that one day you too might be forced down the path that I must travel. She just wants you to be the best prepared by realizing and choosing what is most important in life."

"Loving the king," was Tristan's quiet response.

"Yes, and the realization that as long as you remain loyal, you cannot control the path that is set for you. And your feet must travel the path that is set. Live like this and a strong man you will be, even if someday you must live as I."

A touch from the rain brought Tristan back to the present, and he moved yet again. He hadn't thought about that meeting in years. He had not even thought about his own banishment by Lord Collins in… almost as long. Strange that he should remember this conversation now, though he has found some comfort in this memory. For now, even though he was by himself, he was no longer alone. He took a slow, deep breath; he was no longer alone. Suddenly fire was no longer needed to achieve some comfort here. The comfort soon found an ally in the monotonous drone of the pouring rain, and together they helped his weary mind to float down the wandering path of gentle sleep.

A CHANCE MEETING

They had been watching them approach for quite some time, three hundred armed men marching in their direction. There was nothing for it but to hide in the sparse boulders by the side of the road and hope to remain unseen as these soldiers marched by. There was something almost tragic in being stopped so close to his homeland. He had been telling Jon about all the wondrous sights that his country held; it sounded so good, it even impressed himself. Yes, the biggest disappointment in being taken now would be that his new friend would not see any of it.

The men drew nearer. Suddenly all eyes were turned toward their hiding place. "Well," said Allon, "we tried." As he said this, he turned his head to look back at Jon. But Jon was not there. "Now where…" There he was, stepping out from behind the boulder closest to the road.

"Jon, what have you done?" Even as he was saying this, he watched the leader detach himself from the regiment and approach Jon. Their greeting left no doubt that the two were friends, much to Allon's relief. Indeed, the commander was Jon's comrade and his brother. Not by birth but by bonds, which as Allon would find out, could prove stronger than blood.

These men were currently rushing to the defense of a town in the northern border regions of Eadar. The town of Crioria had come under fierce attack by a people known as the Easi. These were a ferocious people whose warlike history was long and whose preference for attacking the Eadar was strong. This new set of attacks had as their focus the destruction of northern Eadar's cities and towns. Burning the countryside and killing all who lived in their path of destruction, at least killing the fortunate ones. For dark were the practices of the Easi on all who were taken prisoner. For these, death was a pleasant dream.

Crioria had already lost many of its defenders either to death or to capture. These brothers of Jon were now rushing to its defense and to the rescue of those taken captive. This band of men, but three hundred strong, was rushing to face an army of skilled warriors, ones who harbored a bitter hatred for all things of the Eadar.

Allon was very familiar with this northern people, having fought against them on earlier occasions and having walked among them on others. He knew them to be a people who lived in the frigid regions way to the north of Eadar. A people who held little regard for any life, not even their own and that they did indeed have an unreasoning hatred for the Eadarian people. No one knows why there was so much hatred. It had been rumored that it was because of the Eadarian way of life, one marked by freedom. Freedom was an alien concept to the Easi. For them, to live was to rule or be ruled, they did not have personal freedom, they understood it not, and they feared it greatly. Now that is a thought: could it be that their not understanding this freedom created the fear? And since fear was the one thing the Easi could not endure; they sought to eradicate this source of fear by choosing to attack instead of learn? Who knows, perhaps it was nothing more complicated than the cold, in which they lived, had driven all traces of warmth away from their hearts. No one ever knew, and the reason mattered not, for the hatred was very real.

Allon also knew that for all their coldness, they were efficient and cruel fighters. Not many could withstand them. He remembered how even his own army trembled at the mere thought of having to face them on the battlefield and that when his army outnumbered theirs three to one. So, he did not see the sense in these three hundred men rushing to what would be their certain demise and said as much in the council held that evening.

He said, "I know that I am a stranger to all here except Jon. I am honored to be included in this council. Yet, if I may speak…"

"Speak," said the captain.

"Sir, I know the Easi. They are great warriors. You will need at least ten times your number or you march to certain death. I have walked among them in the past and have trained with them. I have even fought against them, and with superior numbers we scarcely held our own. They go mad in the heat of battle. Nothing but their deaths can stop them, and even then, they may find a way to strike at their enemy. They are a cold, vile people, yes. But they are warriors worthy of your deepest respect. Please listen to my council, rather than rush to meet your deaths, go alert your nobles. When they have assembled their armies, then go and fight. Only then will you have a chance to retake your land and free those taken captive."

The commander replied, "That is sound advice. However, to which noble shall we go? Most will not commit to battle, preferring to forfeit the outlying towns and countryside rather than take a stand against those who seek their destruction and hoping that doing so will appease the Easian warlord before their own personal estates suffer the same havoc that is now ravaging their countrymen to the north. They are more worried about themselves than those they are sworn to protect. Those who would fight are engaged elsewhere fighting Brokine's armies. Tell me, to whom shall we go? Who else is there?"

Allon had not been ready for this revelation; it left him unable to respond.

"I am who else," said Jon. "I will go with you."

"This is welcomed news! Will you accept command of half these men?" replied the captain.

"Yes," said Jon.

"This bodes well for us my brothers; our odds are now greatly improved!" shouted the captain to the cheers of all the men.

At this, Allon was taken aback, stunned into silence. First, they were still planning to proceed with this attack. Second, his friend Jon had just been given one-half of the command. There was more to Jon than he knew.

"Captain, you go and defend the town as best you may, I'll go and rescue those taken prisoner," said Jon.

"Done," replied the captain.

Allon, having regained his senses, exclaimed, "Have you not heard what I've said? If you go, there is a very real, a very certain chance that you will not make it back. Do you hear me? You will not make it back!"

"My friend," said Jon, "you know not our king. We have to go. We do not have to make it back."

Allon could find no words to say.

Jon continued, "I am afraid that I will not be able to travel with you to your homeland as I intended. The need of my brothers is too great. I cannot ignore it; I must go. Nor can I ask you to come with us. For as you say, death may be certain. So go in peace, my friend. May there always be a road for you to travel and a song for you to sing." With that, he turned and started to go and make plans for the upcoming defense and rescue.

After a moment, Allon called after Jon, "Wait, I am going with you."

"I cannot ask you to do this thing."

"Yes, well … you are not asking. I am telling."

"Then it is good to have you with us, my friend."

"Yes … besides, you'll not get out of going to my homeland so easily as all that. You promised... and I'm going to see to it that you keep that promise."

"You do that my friend, I truly hope you do."

For the rest of the night, plans were laid. And early the next morning, the two groups of men prepared to part ways, each to their own mission.

"Go with Jubal's guidance," said the captain.

"And you with Jubal's peace and wisdom," came Jon's reply.

Then Jon and Allon watched the first group depart and slowly fade from view. As they faded from sight, Allon broke the silence and asked, "Eadarian, who is Jubal?"

Jon did not answer right away but kept watching the place where his friends had gone. Then with a deep breath, he said, "Our king. Come." With that he started his band of men north to attempt one of the boldest rescues in the history of mankind.

ALONE ON A HILL

Walking alone on a hillside, Corbin pauses for a moment to watch the beauty of a storm rolling in. Corbin loves the weather just prior to a storm, the richness of nature unparalleled. He loves the feel of the wind as it begins to blow, how the green of grass and tree becomes richer than ever before. Then there are the rolling clouds, some black, some white, all in layers ever shifting with no rhyme or reason, but full of depth and power. It is the time when the sky seems most alive.

He stays longer than he should, for he still has some distance to travel. Yet, he doesn't want to leave the comfort he finds here walking alone in the face of the storm. There is something in the billowing of the clouds, in the wave upon wave of wind blown grass, in the incredible pre-storm, darkened lightness that resonates in his soul. It is very tumultuous, yet in it he finds peace. In the coming of the storm, there is something that reminds him that he is not alone, no matter that present circumstances make it appear so.

He takes a long, slow breath, lingers a moment more, then quickens his pace toward shelter. For as much as he loves to watch a storm roll in, he is not overly fond of being caught out in the rain. Nor will we stay and hinder him longer.

YET AGAIN

Frustrating is what it was. Logon had sworn never to allow this to happen again. He had so sworn to friends, family, and even to himself. Yet swearing is a matter of the will, and there are some things that are simply stronger than the will. Not being able to will himself to do what he wants, he does exactly what he does not want to do.

Once again there she is, the most beautiful girl in the world, walking his way, smiling, and looking him right in the eye. He wants to be friendly, he wants to talk to her, he wants her to talk to him, yet against his will, his usual carefree and easygoing manner chooses this most inopportune time to once again vanish more quickly than darkness before candlelight, which leaves him already forgetting how to breathe.

His mind, an advocate of the will, is still clearly focused on what he wants and is now actively engaged in trying to get him to say something, to say anything. It says, "Say hello. Hello. We've rehearsed this; you can do it. Hello." The ensuing silence is deafening. "How about hi? Hi. It is not hard. Hi. Can you please say hi?" Still nothing happens. "Okay, let's just smile, shall we? Smile. Come on smile back at her, you know how. Smile. Will you please smile at the girl! *Arg!* All right, all right, all right… can we at least wave?" But his body ignores the promptings of his mind.

This behavioral plague does not o'ertake him simply because she is beautiful. He has learned that physical beauty can adorn some very ugly people. No, mere physical beauty does not affect him so. But there is something about her that he cannot describe. Something in her eyes, something in her walk, something… well, whatever it is, it has caused him to like her, to like her very much. He likes her so much that his senses leave him whenever she is near.

Which is all very romantic. But it is also quite the royal encumbrance when trying to make conversation. Once again she passes by without him saying a word, not one word. Nor with him giving any indication of how much he genuinely likes her. But as she turns the corner and passes out of sight, his hand does raise to wave. "Oh that's good, real good," speaks his mind. "She might even be impressed...if only she could see you. Well, better late than never, I suppose. Still, it is some progress. Oh, if only I liked her less. At least then I could talk with her." But he likes her so much, so much.

He pauses. *Is it possible to like someone too much to be able to learn to like them better?* He deliberates on this for a moment more, and then shudders from head to toe and quickly continues on his way. Reminding himself that it is still much too early in the day for thoughts such as this. Yes, much, much too early! Sometimes he worries even himself. Though next time, he will speak to her, at least he so swears.

THE RESCUE

Jon and Allon peered down from the ridge as they studied the enemy camp. They had caught up with the Easian prison brigade two days ago, and Jon still did not like what he saw. The brigade numbered five hundred men, only fifty of which were guards for the prisoners. Why the rest were there, he did not know. It really did not matter, for whatever the reason, they were there, and that was going to make the rescue more difficult than anticipated. If it had only been fifty men, he could have easily created some diversion, which would have drawn the guards away from the prisoners, long enough to spirit them away. But what kind of diversion would he need to capture the attention of five hundred men? Five hundred men…

At this point, all but one of his advance scouts had returned. From them he had learned that the current course of the brigade would lead them through a narrow valley about a day's march to the north. He was informed that the far entrance of the valley could be sealed if need be due to a large amount of loose stones and debris found on the slopes at that end and that the near side could be partially blocked off. Also, there was a thick fog that descended ghostlike into the valley at dusk, one so thick that anyone but an arm's length away appeared to be an apparition. Anyone beyond that simply was not seen. The fog, which lingered long after the rising of the sun, imparted an intense feeling of something being dangerously amiss. It was unnerving if for no other reason than because it left them powerless to figure out just what that reason might be. *Perhaps these things could be made to work to our advantage,* thought Jon. He would need all the advantages he could get. His force was now outnumbered more than three to one. So, after posting a watch to keep track of the brigade, he broke camp and moved his men toward the valley.

As they were traveling, they came upon a strange-looking cliff protruding onto the plain. What made it strange was a shelf, which seemed to have been cut into it about halfway up, a shelf whose walls were smooth and polished looking from the shelf floor to cliff top. Jon decided to investigate. Allon found a steep yet accessible path up to the shelf, and once ascended he and Jon found it to be semicircular. On the right, the cliff extended onto the shelf, forming a wall of rock behind which a man could stand and not be seen from below. The wall was indeed polished smooth, and it was very sheer. There were no cracks in this wall, no footholds, no handholds of any kind. As Jon stood admiring the wall, he said half aloud, "I wonder if there is a way up to the top?"

"Yes, there is, sir," came a reply.

Jon quickly spun around to see who had just spoken, for only he and Allon had ascended to the shelf, yet whoever had spoken sounded as if he were standing immediately behind Jon. But no one was there. Jon and Allon exchanged glances, for he had also heard the voice. "Who said that?" asked Jon.

"I did, sir. Down here."

Jon looked down from the shelf, and there at a distance great enough that neither he nor Allon could tell whom it was, stood one of their men. "Amazing," said Allon, marveling at how sound traveled here.

"Yes, it is, sir," was the reply.

"To whom am I speaking?" asked Jon.

"Stillson, sir."

"You know a way to the top of this cliff?"

"Yes, sir. I found it while scouting earlier. That path begins closer to the valley."

"Show it to me when we get there," said Jon.

"Very well, sir."

"Well, you found your way to the top," said Allon. As they turned to go, Allon mused, "You know, the prison brigade will have to pass close enough to here, that if you were so inclined, you could speak to them from this safe distance.

Though, unless you could vanish like a ghost, it would definitely mean your capture."

"Yes," said Jon, as he gazed up the cliff face, "if I could only disappear. Come, we have far to go."

They started to descend from the shelf, when suddenly they were stopped in their tracks by a sound unlike any they had ever heard before. It was coming from above their heads. It was a mournful, ghastly, and haunting howl. No creature of which they were aware could make such a sound, no matter how much pain it was in. Instantly Jon's men were on alert, swords in hand. Jon gave orders for a search party. If that were a living creature, it was in dire need. If not, they needed to know what they now faced. His men were just beginning to fan out when Stillson came running up. "Sir, there is no need to send the men. I can tell you what that is."

"Speak quickly," said Jon.

"On top of that cliff is a strange bunch of reeds. When the wind blows across them, they make that ghastly sound."

"Reeds?" asked Jon. "Are you sure?"

"Yes, sir. I was on top of the cliff and just

stepped past them on my way to the edge when a breeze began to blow. I spun around with sword in hand yet nothing but the reeds was present. I went back and looked at them more closely, I even broke one off and tied it to a bit of rope and spun it around my head; just to make sure it was the reeds. It made that same sound, sir."

Jon gazed back at the top of the cliff. "Reeds? Stillson, you're the scout that didn't make it back before we broke camp, aren't you?"

"Yes, sir."

"Good, come with me and make your report. I want to know everything."

The rest of Stillson's report simply confirmed the information that the other scouts had provided. So once again Jon started moving toward the valley. Upon their arrival at the valley, Jon promptly left with Stillson to find the way to the top of the cliff, leaving Allon to set up camp and more thoroughly scout the valley. Jon thought he should be back before dusk. But he was not. Nor had he returned by the time the fog descended upon the valley. The fog was so thick that Allon could not see more than a foot in any direction.

This fog was also unnaturally cold; Allon felt a chill in his very bones. He gave up all hopes of seeing Jon until the fog lifted the next day. There would be no way Jon could find them in this. He checked the watch and had just turned to retire for the evening when he left the ground, inspired by the coldest, eeriest wailing he had ever heard. When the sound died, he heard Jon's familiar laugh. His first response was, "Good! He made it back." His second: "Now I'm going to kill him."

Jon came forward and said, "I am truly sorry for scaring you. But now I know it will work. It will work!"

"What will work?" asked Allon, with more than a little edge to his voice as he was not overly convinced about the sincerity of Jon's apology.

"Our diversion," was Jon's reply. Quickly he laid out for Allon what he had in mind.

When Jon finished, Allon said, "That is insane. You know this, completely insane. But it is so much so that it might just work."

"It's settled then," said Jon. "Let's inform the men."

For the rest of that night, plans were made.

Cobal stood and watched the brigade prepare for another day's march. He had not wanted to command this brigade; there was no glory in it. He would much rather be back on the front, razing that wretched village to the ground. That would be worthy of praise, not to mention vastly more satisfying. But it was his turn in rotation and he could not say no. He would simply have to endure this a while longer. Besides, there was sure to be more fighting and more glory to be gained. Nor was this trip entirely without its merits. He was taking immense pleasure in the mistreatment of the prisoners.

When all was ready, he gave the order, and the brigade began another long day's march. But it was at this point that boredom ceased. For suddenly a loud, mournful, and bone-chilling wail pierced the morning air. Cobal had never heard anything like it before, nor could he imagine what could possibly make such a sound. He began barking orders. Sending men to scour the countryside, he wanted to find and destroy whatever it was. Yet, just as the men started toward the sound, it stopped. Then it started again farther down the ridge. Much farther than anything could have run in such a short period of time. Was there more than one of those things? "Go!" shouted Cobal. The men departed.

Time passed. The morning passed and no one returned. Midday came and mid-afternoon went, and still no one reported back; though the howling could still be heard dancing along the ridge. It was only as night finally approached that the men started to return. Eventually all the men returned, all but two. Those two were never seen again. Those that returned reported to their commander, "We could not find the source of that ghastly howl, sire."

"You could find nothing?" roared Cobal.

"Begging the commander's pardon, sire, but that is why we are so long in returning. We wanted to have something to tell you. But whenever we arrived at where the source of the howling should have been, there was simply nothing there. No tracks, no signs of life ... nothing. Then the sound would start farther off. Thinking we had gone to the wrong location, we would run to the new one, only to meet with the same results. As the day progressed, we split up hoping that in doing so we would stand a better chance of finding the source of that haunting cry. But nothing, sire, nothing. Also, Huddelston and Ericson are missing." Silent and tense moments passed.

"Dismissed," snapped Cobal.

"Thank you, sire."

Cobal was more than annoyed. A full day wasted, and he still had no answers. He had lost two men; and worse than that, he had heard his men talking about how unearthly that sound was. Without an answer, their minds would come up with all sorts of wild imaginings. He knew that such imaginings only served to give unreasoning fear a foothold and that such fear would be a far worse enemy than whatever was out there making that noise. He would start posting scouts and sentries. He must find ways to keep his men busy, to keep their minds off the unknown. Yet as he was thinking this, the cry tore through the air once again, this time much closer to camp. "Just how am I going to keep their minds off that?" asked Cobal.

Before the break of day, they were on the

move. He had decided to move and move quickly. He wanted to make the shore and be at sea as soon as possible. He hoped that the brisk routine of a forced march would keep his men focused on their tasks and off that mysterious and haunting noise. He also hoped that by moving, they would leave behind whatever it was making that haunting cry. But that was not to be. The soul-piercing cry seemed at first to follow, then to lead, then to mark time beside them. Yet still they pressed on. Always alert, always on guard. When suddenly, the men spotted something and shouted for their captain. Cobal went to see what they had found.

There in the distance a man was standing on a ledge. Standing erect with hands folded, as if he were waiting for someone. *Here at last is something tangible for the men to do,* thought Cobal. He ordered every one forward. As they approached, the man on the shelf made no move. He stood still, so still that he might have been made of stone. As they drew close, Cobal heard a strange voice ordering them to, "Stop!" He looked up, and the man had now extended his hand, palm out, and repeated the order, "Stop now!"

What kind of magic was this, that he could

hear this man over such a great distance? He responded, "Who are you that you order me to stop?"

"I am the lord of the mists," came the reply from overhead. "Progress no further, or you will all die."

"I am Cobal, commander of this Easian prison brigade. No one gives me orders, not without an army to support him. I see no such army."

"But you have heard them," was the reply. And the terrible howling screamed through the air once more.

"What are you?" shouted Cobal. "Have your army show itself now or this discussion is over and you are a dead man!"

"Now you begin to understand." Laughed the man. "I am the lord of the mists that reside in the valley."

"Ghosts, do you mean ghosts?"

"Mists, ghosts, it matters not what you call us. Enter into the valley, and you will belong to us."

"You don't look like a ghost. You look like a living man."

Laughter again erupted from the man of the

shelf. "What do ghosts look like? But I tell you this, enter into the valley, and the ghosts will look like you." With that the one on the ledge moved slightly to his right, vanishing from view.

Cobal ordered his men to the ledge. "Bring him to me! Alive. He may become battered and beaten on the way back, but I want him alive. We will see how well his wit serves him with his hands bound and his face bloodied."

The men charged, racing up to the ledge. They were eager to grab and bind the one who had taunted them so. But the man was not there. There was no one on the ledge. The cliff walls were solid, smooth, and impossibly tall. There was no place a man could hide or have escaped to. But... he was not here. They turned and the commander asked, "Well, where is he?"

"He is not here, sire. There is nowhere he could have gone, but he is simply not here. It is like he never was."

"You're not telling me he was a ghost, are you?"

Before the man could answer, the piercing howl commenced yet again. But this time, instead of being the solitary voice they had heard earlier, there were now many, many horrifying voices. It was more than unnerving. Even to the commander, who did not believe in such things as ghosts.

Then suddenly there was silence, dreadful, imposing, complete silence, a silence that went beyond the mere stoppage of the cries. It was hard to know which was worse. At least with the howling there was something to guard against. "Form up!" shouted the captain. They would enter that valley. They would enter it, and woe be unto anyone who got in their way.

Now, while Cobal takes time arranging his men into battle formations, let us take notice of something that he could not. Upon saying, "…the ghosts will look like you." The "ghost" stepped to the right, behind the wall of rock, and out of sight of the soldiers below. He then quickly put his arms through loops in the ropes, which were then hanging down the cliff face. With a quick jerk on the rope as a signal, he was swiftly hauled up. Yet, even with all possible haste in this ascent, he barely cleared the top of the cliff when the soldiers stormed the ledge. Upon regaining his feet, he waited for the proper moment and then signaled his men. Reeds began to spin. Creating a noise so loud and wrenching that he nearly became a ghost in actuality. Moments passed, another signal, the cries stopped, and the men withdrew. "Will that stop them Eadarian?" asked Allon.

"No," said Jon. "But it will make them uncertain. Come, we must hurry."

They ran back to the valley to make final preparations for the rescue.

When the brigade arrived at the entrance to the valley, their muscles tensed. Caution now slowed their movements. But they were ready for the attack, the one that never came. Because of this slower progress, the last of the Easian brigade did not enter the valley until just prior to dusk. They traveled only a little way into the valley, because even though he did not want to, Cobal ordered camp to be made. It was fast approaching night, and it would be far worse to continue traveling through this unfamiliar valley and risk losing some of his men to the dark rather than waiting until morning. He doubled the nightly guard.

It was then that the ghostlike fog descended upon the valley. Slowly it became thicker and thicker until the men were isolated from anyone more than a foot or so away. The men were nervous and on edge; they were in a situation not to their liking, not knowing who the enemy was or how to fight them. Then just as the fog became its thickest, two great rumblings reached their ears, one from up ahead and one from behind. Then once again there was complete silence. Cobal, suspecting what had just occurred, swore somewhat less than softly. They were now sealed in. He could not risk scouts at this time. He would need them when the attack came. The blocked passageways would simply have to wait until the morning.

The waiting game was on and time was on Jon's side. "The longer they have to wait, the more the odds are tipped in our favor," is how Jon explained it to Allon and the men. In preparation for the rescue, a handful of men had been stationed at the far entrance of the valley to help create the needed diversion. Jon had then handpicked thirty-two men to join himself and Allon in infiltrating the Easian camp. Of these he choose two to join him and Allon to help with the actual freeing of the prisoners. All the remaining men were then hidden among the debris at the valley's near end. Some were hidden so close to the path that when the brigade passed by, they were but a sword's length away.

The plan was as follows. Jon's thirty-four men were split in half and posted on opposite sides of the valley with directions to keep pace with the brigade as it progressed northward. This was so the brigade could be surrounded quickly when they stopped for the night. Then, after the fog set in, ever so often one of the thirty-four would briefly spin his reed. It was even better if two or more happened to spin them at the same time. But it was only to be the briefest of spins and always, always there had to be a long silence following any of the spins. Jon hoped that this would make sleep for the Easi impossible, that it would keep this enemy off their balance; thus improving the odds in his favor, even if ever so slightly. Then on Jon's signal, a long spinning of his reed, the rescue would begin. Then Jon and his party, four in number, would make their way to the prisoners as the other thirty men were infiltrating the camp, spinning their reeds, stopping, then swiftly and quietly moving to another position and spinning them anew. They were to continue doing so, thereby creating the impression that an entire army of shrieking ghosts was invading the camp. To add to this diversion, those at the far end of the valley, at this same signal from Jon, were to light a series of large bon fires, this to serve two purposes. First, he was hopeful that the firelight would draw the enemy soldiers to it and away form the prisoners. Second, it was a point of reference for the rescuers, thus preventing them from getting lost in the fog. Once Jon and Allon had "spirited" the captives safely away, all the men that had remained hidden would stand and spin their reeds in unison, sounding the call for disengagement and retreat.

With luck, it would be much later, after the fog eventually lifted the next day, before the prisoners would be missed. Jon hoped that the Easi would then think that the horde of the mist had spirited them away and so believing, not give chase. However, if not and there was pursuit, well, there was no planning for if not. There would be no choice but to fight to the death, and as it has been said, the odds were not in Jon's favor.

That was the plan, and now, in the morning's darkest hours, it was time to begin. Jon rose and spun his reed long and loud. When he did so, the other thirty-three stood and spun theirs, the fires were lit, and the rescue was on. With that initial ghastly chorus, the enemy camp came to its feet, swords in hand, ready to strike at the source of their fear. As the wailing continued moving freely through the fog, the men became more edgy, became more and more eager to strike at something, at anything, so much so, that when a reed was spun close behind one of the Easian warriors, he spun wildly, striking blindly with his sword. He missed the reed spinner but struck and killed a fellow soldier, whose dying scream proved too much for the strained nerves of some, and they too started striking out at whatever was closest. Mayhem and madness prevailed as fear and fog mixed in the confused minds of the

Easian soldiery. It was in this fashion that they unknowingly began to attack each other. Soon the clash of swords was heard through out the camp, which spawned even greater clashes of swords. For now the fear of attack was being realized and more and more men were rushing to the defense of themselves. Cobal and the men closest to him realized what was happening and tried to regain control, to reestablish order, only to be set upon by those too fear driven to hear their words. Cobal now found himself fighting for his life against his own men.

Jon's group of four found the going slow. The fog was thick, and they did not want to share in the mass of confusion that had been unleashed in the Easian camp. Even so, their progress toward the prison area was without incident until someone, running very hard, smashed directly into Jon, causing both to fall. Quickly the two scrambled to their feet. Jon now stood eye to eye with Cobal. "You!" shouted Cobal, and he lunged. Jon barely evaded the blow and quickly drew his own sword. "You are responsible for what is happening to my men," spewed Cobal.

"I warned you not to come here," said Jon. "You would not listen. Now you will pay dearly for your arrogance."

"I will not be the only one who pays this day," vowed the Easian commander.

He charged, and blades clashed, with the swords gleaming eerily in the dim glow caused by the signal fires. Though the gleam was short lived, it died as each blade quickly became covered in blood. It was a savage battle, a fight for life in which no quarter was asked and none given, one in which primal strength and emotion waged a desperate contest for life. It was a battle that only one could win; the other must fall. The wounds he inflicted were too shallow and those he received, too deep; soon he breathed no more. The other knelt, leaned for support upon his sword, and gasped for air. Allon rushed in, "Eadarian!"

"I'm all right," said Jon. Then he took time to catch his breath.

Allon did not think it safe to wait too long and said, "Come, there will be others."

"Yes," said Jon. "Let's finish this." His attention then turned from the fallen commander back to those held captive.

Already the sounds of fighting were dying away and to their amazement and relief, they found the prisoners unguarded. Jon wasted no time. Keeping the signal fires to their backs, he started the prisoners toward freedom. When they were all away, the retreat was sounded. Jon then hurried his men to quickly put as much distance as he could between them and the Easi. They traveled for a day and a half before Jon called a halt to their march. Here they would rest until those now free had regained some of their strength. Also, they had just pulled off an incredible feat, the prisoners were free, and there was no pursuit. A little celebration was called for. Jon was proud of his men and what they had accomplished. Being down three to one against the Easi and coming out victorious was something unheard of, something miraculous, something…worthy of remembrance.

The next two days passed swiftly, and Allon saw little of Jon, who was busy tending to those who had become ill and wounded under the "tender" care of the Easi. He was also assessing the combat readiness of those well enough to fight. They were now making ready to head back to the embattled town of Crioria, the hometown of these rescued men; and since it may yet be under attack, this was something he needed to know.

On the third day, Allon did not see Jon around the camp. After looking around, he found Jon sitting on a big boulder, which overlooked a fast-running creek. Jon was so somber and contemplative that he was unaware of Allon's approach. "Contemplating the defense of Crioria?" Allon asked.

"No" was Jon's quiet reply.

"Is everything all right?"

"Yes."

"For a man who single-handedly felled a great Easian commander, you don't seem very excited. And may I remind you, that is no small feat?" said Allon.

"Thank you," said Jon. "I have not forgotten. It's just a great Eadarian law at work."

"Law?" asked Allon.

"The more loyal you stay to the king, the more like him you begin to think."

Allon thought about this and then very intellectually said, "Huh?"

Jon continued, "Allon, do you ever wonder about those who have fallen by your sword? Do they leave behind a wife, family, someone who will miss them and mourn their passing? Take that commander, what did he do before becoming a soldier? Did he have hopes and dreams of doing other things? Was he truly an evil man? If not, what lies had he been told; how was hate fostered to make him come so far from home to die?"

"He was Easian, he was your enemy. That is all the thought there need be," scoffed Allon.

"Is it? He was the enemy yes, but he was also a man."

"Who said he wasn't? You're not going to get all teary eyed over a fallen enemy, are you?" asked an incredulous Allon.

"No. Do not misunderstand me, Allon. I am not saddened by the victory; of that I am excited and proud. It was well done."

"Yes, it was," replied Allon.

"But I am saddened by the fact that there *had*

to be one," continued Jon. "The need for such victories is a great evil that walks among men."

Allon solemnly nodded his head, thought about this for a moment, then quite profoundly said, "Huh?"

"Come," said Jon, with a hint of laughter in his eyes. "Crioria may still be under attack, and if so, its need will now be dire. If not and all is well, a real celebration will begin when these who were prisoners are returned home. Either way, we should not keep that town waiting."

Allon, who was now scratching his head and hadn't really heard this last comment said, "Huh?"

Grinning, Jon responded, "Come; fighting or revelry is our next destination."

"Why didn't you just say so?" said Allon, greatly relieved at this change of topic.

"Come, my friend," laughed Jon. "We have far to go."

By midday, Jon and his men were on the move, headed for Crioria.

The great Eadarian rescue was now complete.

CORBIN AND THE WIDOW MIMMS

It all occurred because of Widow Mimms or, rather, because of the widow's situation. You see, Widow Mimms was well on in years. Indeed, no one knew for sure which had come first, the surrounding mountains or Widow Mimms. However, for all that, there was still a fire in her eyes and purpose in her steps. Yet as able bodied as she was, her body was not as able as it used to be. For example, hitching up the team and driving to town for supplies was no longer something she could do for herself.

Until recently, her neighbor Malcom had always stopped by on his weekly trip to town and brought back whatever she might need. However, Malcom had recently been inconsiderate enough so as to get himself trampled by a bull. Fortunately he only broke his leg and a couple of ribs and was recuperating nicely at his sister's house in town. In a few months, he would be as good as new. But for the time being, this did make his weekly trips something other than possible. Happily for the widow, she lived near a town full of kindhearted people. When her plight was revealed; more than enough volunteers came forward to make these supply runs. And today was Corbin's day.

Corbin was in good spirits this day. He was feeling good about helping Widow Mimms, about this ride into the country, about life in general. Most specifically though, he was feeling good about the Midsummer's Dance that was being held that night, rather, about dancing with Sarah. He could think of little else. Even while loading the wagon and covering the supplies, he was thinking about the dance and not really focusing on what he was doing. This did slow him down a little, but it was a great day. He had plenty of time; why rush? When all was ready, he climbed into the driver's seat, inhaled very deeply, and turned the horses toward the open road.

He had been looking forward to this dance for many weeks, and he couldn't even dance. To say that he had two left feet is being rather kind. But Sarah *could* dance, and she was the most intoxicatingly beautiful girl he had ever known. Now, for her part, Sarah did not care that Corbin could not dance; she cared for Corbin. They would be together, and that was enough for her.

As I said, he was thinking about this as he loaded the wagon. He was thinking about this as he started the horses down the road. He was thinking about this as the horses made their own way and set their own pace to the widow's house. He was still dreaming of the dance, of Sarah, when suddenly he was overcome with the feeling that something was terribly, terribly wrong. Have you ever been so captivated by what you were thinking that it takes a few moments to become aware of what is actually happening around you? This is what was happening to Corbin. He sat there and looked around, then looked around again, and yet again. But he just couldn't figure out what was wrong. He was even about to dismiss the feeling when a sudden rush of realization overcame him. He wasn't moving. The horses had stopped dead in their tracks.

It is truly amazing how quickly the human mind can pass from thought to thought and from emotion to emotion. All much quicker than a sailor can be caused to curse. Yes, even faster than that, I assure you. And just that fast, Corbin went from a heavenly romantic bliss to something not short of vehement disgust.

In front of him was an impassable chasm. The space he faced was not more than fifteen feet deep and no more than fifty feet wide, and there was a strong and fast river at its base. Okay, it was not really a chasm, but it may as well have been one for he had no way to cross it. And he was disgusted about being here. What bothered him most was the fact that he knew this impasse was here. This was where the road used to cross the Black River. But the extra heavy rains and the resulting floods of this past spring had washed out the bridge. He had even been here since then. The first time to just look at the wreckage, the next few times were to help in the clean up, recovery, and preparation for a new bridge. A bridge, he had known was still not built. Yet here he was. But he had been thinking about Sarah. Still, he was now behind schedule, and the dance would wait for no man.

Luckily for Corbin, he was a man who could clearly assess any situation and then quickly reach a decision. Of even greater fortune was his boldness in taking action based on that decision. First and foremost, he decided that he was extremely happy that neither Sarah nor any of his friends were here to witness this. Second, he very rapidly decided that they would never find out. And third, that he must quicken his pace in reaching the next bridge, which was a few miles away. He hurried on. Even so, he knew he would be lucky to make it to the dance on time.

It is at this point that it began to rain. At first it was a light rain, more of a misty drizzle than an actual rain. The kind that is just enough to keep one's clothing damp and clammy without ever bringing the freedom of being so wet that it no longer mattered. Corbin took a deep breath to help keep his calm. Once he got to the dance, all this would matter not. After all, even if he were slightly late, he could still dance with Sarah for most of the evening. And look, there was the second bridge! Yes, now he was sure he would make it for most of the dance. He crossed the bridge at a fast trot.

He had just crossed the bridge when someone heard his complaints about not being truly wet and answered with a vengeance. It started raining so hard that Corbin could no longer see the road while sitting in the driver's seat. With the widow's house being the closest shelter, he had no choice but to keep moving. Now, to keep the wagon from ending up in a ditch, he had to climb down and lead the horses. Needless to say, this slowed his progress. One might say that he was no longer a happy man, nor did he find much freedom in being so thoroughly wet.

Eventually the rain did slacken, and he was able to climb back into the driver's seat, more than a little eager to hurry on his way. By the time he now got home, the dance would be more than half over. *Well, some dancing will be better than no dancing,* he thought. Then the thunder rolled in with claps so loud that they seemed to happen just overhead and proved momentarily deafening. This spooked the horses, and his newly set faster pace became an all-out sprint for life, Corbin's life. It was all he could do just to hang on. The horses were running wild, and they were still madly running as they took the wrong turn at the fork in the road. By the time the horses had calmed down enough for Corbin to slow them down and get them turned around, too much time had been lost. There was no way he was going to make it back to town before the dance was long over.

What a waste of an evening! He started to think this as he made the turn that would take him to Widow Mimms'. Corbin, who was both thoroughly wet and starting to get cold, now had plenty of time to contemplate what he was missing. There would be no dance, no time with Sarah. This should have been so easy. This was to have been so simple and so quick. Why, why do these things happen to him? He had planned this evening for over a month; dance all night, a quiet stroll to her house with even quieter whispers. Whispers about anything…everything…nothing at all. Listening to the music of her laughter. Then perhaps, just perhaps…a goodnight kiss. "All that planning for nothing. What a waste. What a complete and utter waste of my day!" shouted Corbin, just prior to pulling in sight of the widow's house.

He continued thinking such thoughts as he pulled into the widow's yard. He was in no mood to talk to anyone. Perhaps he could simply set all the supplies on the porch and just leave. She would find them in the morning. It wouldn't hurt anything he had brought if they sat by the door all night. The more he thought this over the more appealing it became. He pulled up to her door and had just finished unloading when he heard a sound that made him cringe—the opening of the front door. Would none of his plans go well today? He took a deep breath and slowly exhaled, and then turned to greet Widow Mimms. As he turned around he was determined to politely as possible say hello, ask where she wanted everything, then take his leave and hurry home.

Yet, he had no sooner turned to face the widow then he became motionless, captivated by the biggest and most genuine smile that he had ever seen. There stood Widow Mimms, smiling from ear to ear and from eye to eye. She thanked him for coming all that way and "...in such nasty weather too," she said. "It must be hard on a young man to have to travel so far, become soaking wet, and then miss the chance to dance with all the pretty girls."

This caught Corbin off guard, and at his sustained silence she asked, "Or is there one particular girl?"

In spite of himself, Corbin blushed. The widow kept on smiling, "Oh yes, young man, I know all about the dance. Used to go when I was younger. You know what I always liked best? The quiet strolls home with my young man. Whispering about everything and about nothing, all at the same time... but that was a long time ago. Why, where are my manners? Will you do me the honor of staying for dinner?"

Corbin stood there, wide-eyed in silence. "Yes, I know it is late," continued the widow. "But put your horses in the barn, then come in and dry off. I suspect that warm cider and some hot stew will feel mighty good to a body that's been caught out in the rain." With that, she turned and went inside to prepare him dinner.

Corbin turned and led the horses to the barn. *There will be other dances,* he sighed, *and Sarah will enjoy hearing all about this evening... No, not all about it, only about the things I will be able to live down.* As I said, he was a quick decision maker. Then as he rubbed down his horses, he thought, *All right, I guess today has been worthwhile after all. Yes, it has after all.* When the horses were taken care of, Corbin went back to the house. He paused only for a second as he reached the front porch to look up to contemplate the night sky. *And if my luck holds... it will rain all the way home.* He then turned his attention to carrying the supplies inside, ready to enjoy whatever dinner Widow Mimms had prepared.

PATIENCE

Corbin was hiding in the underbrush, the densely woven branches in which he was concealed shielded him well from enemy eyes, if not from the pouring rain, and it was raining now, quite steadily. Yet to move would be to die, for members of an opposing clan had been hunting him for more than a day and a half. They had been getting close, and it was only this last ditch effort at concealment that, for now, had saved him. As they were closing in, he had dismounted from his horse and slapped it on the rear end, which sent it running for home. He hoped that the pursuit would follow the tracks of the galloping horse and so pass by his hiding place, which would leave him both unnoticed and alive. So far it seemed to be working. Now he simply had to wait… to wait. Strange are the things brought to ones memory at times like these. Some have remembered the greatest moments of their lives, others their greatest pain. All that Corbin called from memory… was merely having wished for just a little more patience.

It had all started on the day he found that he would be able to go home this year to celebrate the Great Dawning, his country's biggest holiday, the festival of its founding. He was so excited, as much about going home as by the celebration itself. He even ordered brand-new cloths to be worn at the festivities. He planned to leave the day the clothes were ready; his plans had been so simple. He would pick them up early and then leisurely take the rest of that day and the next two in traveling home. This would allow him to enjoy the journey and arrive in time to spend a couple of days with family and friends before the celebration began. It had been such a good plan. Why is it that plans and reality so often part ways?

When he had gone to pick up the clothes, he found they had been made too small. The tailor was very sorry for having made such a mistake, yet all the apologies in the world could not make the clothes ready before midmorning of the next day. This delay was unexpected and unwelcomed, but what could he do? He would just have to travel faster than he planned but at least he could still arrive when he wanted. But then the next day, when the appointed time finally arrived, he found it would be later still before everything was ready. A delay of more than a day and a half and the distance between here and home was not getting any shorter. He had the rest of the day to contemplate this and the more he thought about it, the more agitated he became, for all his plans seemed to becoming undone.

When he finally took delivery of his clothes and all was ready, it was later than late afternoon and Corbin was in a great rush to leave. Indeed, he was thinking of nothing else. He wanted to get on his horse and go! He was bound and determined to make up some lost time before stopping that night. So he jumped upon his horse, kicked it, and whipped it hard thinking, *Let the race home begin!* Now, Corbin's horse was strong, spirited, very fast, and one unused to such accommodations. So instead of racing down the street as Corbin had in mind, he turned his head, looked up at Corbin, and commenced in letting his displeasure be known. Corbin's conscience became terribly troubled, rather abruptly, at having caused his horse so much discomfort, so abruptly that he strongly vowed never again to treat his horse in this manner, no matter how great his sense of urgency. Now, as has been said elsewhere, Corbin had the ability to make decisions quickly, and this one was reached in the blink of an eye as his gaze was turned skyward while reposing flat on his back with the horse standing over him, looking down with a slight cock of its head as if to ask, "What were you thinking?"

Corbin climbed back to his feet and while scratching his horse's nose as way of apology said,

"I really should not have lost my temper over this. I do wish that I'd have had more patience."

Suddenly he was back in the present as his muscles tensed. Was that the sound of a twig snapping under foot? His hand grasped his knife; this work would be up close and personal. Long moments went by with no other sound, without any other hint of movement. He was grateful for that. His hiding place had been well chosen, with twigs and brush everywhere around. An enemy could not approach with out his arrival being announced well before he came into view.

Eventually the rain did stop. Corbin still remained poised and silent, alert for any that might discover his hiding place. He waited patiently as darkness fell. He even waited until dawn the next day, many hours after going into hiding, before he chose to emerge from the brush. Even then he stayed low, kept close to the ground, and scouted around for any sign of the enemy. Soon he found it; they had been very close. Indeed, in better weather, they may have found him. But now they were gone.

He then stood, and the tension slowly

drained from his muscles. They had not found him and he was now free to proceed at his leisure. He decided to take time to watch the sun rise upon the distant western mountains. As he did so, he began to think on the great irony that would soon be taking place. His new suit of cloths, which were still on his horse, would be arriving in time for the Great Dawning, and he... he would be worse than late. He shook his head and began the long walk home. Though he did choose at this moment to make another decision, quite swiftly, *He would never, never, never wish for patience, not ever again!*

THE RITE

No one remembered how Power Falls received its name. It certainly wasn't because of the amount of water that came over the top. Then it would have been named Constant Falls, Steady Falls, or perhaps Peaceful Falls. However, the massive promontory over which the water fell did emit a sense of grandeur and power. Perhaps that was the reason. No one knew, and really it mattered not. Not to Nathan, who was standing at the base of the falls. It only mattered that he was on a mission, one that required him to reach the top of this waterfall. And since there was no other way he could ascend, he began climbing the winding path before him.

Mission. Nathan had to laugh at himself. For *mission* was much too strong a word for what he was to accomplish this day. He was merely climbing to the top of this rock face in order to stand at the head of the falls and look out over the valley. That was all. That was the mission. He had simply come home to complete this rite of passage.

When Nathan was a boy, growing up in this valley, there had been several rites of passage for young boys to go through on their way to manhood. "Rites of passage" sounds daunting, does it not? But these rites were not tests to prove manhood; rather, they were celebrations of arrival into it. For even as a man would not run a marathon without being fully prepared, a rite would not be given until it was well known that the boy was man enough to pass it.

The climbing of Power Falls had been one of these rites. To pass, the youths had to ascend to the top of this promontory, a climb of over four hundred feet. They scaled it by means of a long, narrow, and jagged path that twisted along its face. Once they reached the summit, at the head of the falls, they would stand in front of their chief while he ceremoniously drew water from the creek, poured it over their heads, and said, "The water flows over you now, even as it flows over the mighty cliff you have just ascended. You have gained the strength of the rock. You have ascended to the power needed for manhood. Well done! Let us now continue your journey." He would then turn and lead a solemn procession back to town, this in order to remind the boys that manhood was a journey and not a destination. Then the whole village would hold a gathering and celebrate the boy's success.

Now the path was not that harrowing, nor overly difficult, but one needed to be more than a child to have the stamina to scale it. It was the only rite Nathan had never passed. Not that he did not have the strength to pass, but... well, he would always make it about halfway up, to a point where the path doubled back upon itself quiet sharply. When it did this, the path opened into a majestic view, with the whole valley spreading out before the climber: the mountains in the distance, the great river, their village with all its little houses, and a very unobstructed view to the base of the falls. One became acutely aware of how incredibly far it was to the bottom. To Nathan, this awareness was...ah...cute? No. And it would indeed be a powerful fall. Though it wasn't the possibility of falling that had bothered him, it was the certainty of landing. He never quite got over that certainty. But that had been many years ago, several lifetimes ago. No one had ever questioned his ability to be a man, nor had any thought that he would be a mere grown up, an aged boy. So why was he here? This was something he had to do, for himself.

So he placed one foot in front of the other. It was not quite as steep as he remembered, though it was just as slippery. But he moved up the path with relative ease, at least until he saw the bend, that infamous twist in the path. He stopped, wondered if he was being foolish, shook his head, and then continued on. Slowly he rounded the turn and kept his eyes up and on the cliff, only on the cliff. He took three more steps like this and then stopped. He knew he had to look. His ascension would be incomplete if he failed to look this fear straight in the eye. So, he closed his eyes, slowly turned, and leaned back into the cliff wall; his hands clutched tightly the holds they had found. Only then, once secure, did he allow his eyes to open.

It was a magnificent view. The mountains, purple in the distance, the lush green of the valley, and the mighty river winding on its way as it raced to meet those mountains. It was breathtaking. It was so magnificent that he found himself wondering why he couldn't do this when he was younger. Then he lowered his gaze... and remembered. Even though he was only halfway up the falls, it was a long way to the bottom, and that pool of water at the base would not make for a soft landing. Now as has been said, many years had passed since he was a youngster trying to celebrate his coming of age. And they have not all been easy years, and he has passed through perils far more hair raising and severe than this possibility of pain.

That was why he refused to stop, as he had when a boy, and return the way he had come. He was still not in love with the view to the bottom and the possibility of falling was still very real. Yet it was not the looming reality it was in his youth. Turning, he continued the ascent. If anything, the path became easier and soon all sight of the bottom was lost from view as the path continued to twist, turn, and climb. The rest of the climb passed quickly. Then having gained the top; he knelt at the water's edge, scooped up two handfuls, and let it pour over his head. He savored this moment for he had finally passed this rite of manhood. True, there was no one here to see it done and there would be no cheering crowds to help celebrate. But what it meant to him to stand here at the edge of the falls and look out over the valley while the water dripped from his hair was … beyond description. But he felt good, very, very good. Yes, this had been meaningless act, but it was not a pointless one.

He stayed a moment longer then turned and started for home.

Well done, Nathan. Well done!

DIFFERENT DRUMMER

J on has always walked to the cadence of a different drummer. Rarely was this a planned or ever intentional; mostly he was simply being his own man. For instance, when most loved being in crowds and avoided being alone, he loved solitary walks along the ragged, windblown cliffs and the solemn cries of a passing gull. He was aware that most thought this strange. For they preferred the safety offered by the towns and villages and ventured forth from these safe havens only at times of dire need. Not Jon. It is not that Jon disdained crowds. Indeed, he welcomed any who would join him on his walks through the wild hills. Yet, he felt no compulsion to wait for anyone either and often roamed the wild hills alone, finding solace in the solitude. If you were looking for a neat classification or label to place on Jon … it has been tried before, and none has ever been found. Though it has been said that while others were properly worrying about their future, with what it would hold, with whom it would bring. Jon was too busy enjoying life each and every day, one day at a time.

Usually that was enough for Jon, not so today. Today he and Allon had just come from the gathering of a clan where the praise was sung of all that he was not. The praise of a life that was not in keeping with Jon's character; one he could not live up to. It was the praise of all those who march to the same drummer, the same beat, and the exact same rhythm.

Normally this did not bother Jon. But today, he was no longer sure that he liked the rhythms his drummer had been playing. So much so that even the none-too-perceptive Allon took note of Jon's melancholy, which caused him to ask the deeply moving question, "What is wrong with you?"

"Oh, I don't know," said Jon.

"I have found that such not knowing tends to have its roots in the knowing."

"Did anyone ever tell you that you are the epitome of compassion?"

"Now that you mention it, yes."

"They lied."

"But I am right," said Allon.

"Well…maybe," said Jon. "It's just that all those people listed, those praised as being the greatest contribution to our society, as being a source of pride for clan and king. Were all masters of one vocation and all were married, or had been, and had raised a fine family. I'm none of that."

In truth, Jon wasn't even close to truly mastering any craft or vocation. Oh, he knew a little about a great many things and a large amount concerning a select few; indeed he has done more and seen more in his lifetime than most would if given two. Yet he had mastered nothing. When he was a younger man, he had been interested in so many things that he could not limit himself to learning just one. As for a wife, well, he had always more or less assumed that one day it would happen. But it had never been the all out driving force, the passion that it had been for others, like those on the list. He'd been content with enjoying his life as it unfolded. He lived it to the fullest. Ah, now there's a thought. Perhaps Jon had mastered something after all; perhaps he had mastered the craft of living well.

But Jon was not thinking of this. "Allon, am I really living wisely, honestly pursuing the dream of my king? Or has my life been a lie to which my "different rhythm" merely made me blind?"

Allon paused, thought for a second, then took a deep breath and said rather astutely, "Huh?" Then he continued, "What is wrong with you today? You have heard all this many times before and it has never bothered you."

"I know," said Jon, "but sometimes…sometimes I wonder if, since so many different chiefs say the same things, isn't it possible that I am in the wrong? That I've messed up, wasted my life, and that perhaps now it is too late to…to have what the others have?"

"Ah," said Allon. "Feeling old and lonely, are we?"

"You can choose to remain silent," replied Jon.

"Yes, but why would I do that?"

"Why? Why do I bother?"

"Come on," said Allon, in a tone that was not unlike laughter.

"Where?"

"How is it, you say? Ah yes, 'When our minds run up against a rock wall, it is then time to put the body in motion to scale it,'" here Allon paused with a big grin smeared all over his face.

Jon groaned. It was bad enough to be hit with Allon's sardonic wit, but now to also have one of his own sayings used against him…life really wasn't playing fair. "You are looking way too smug. You know this, don't you?"

"Yes. I know. Well come on, granny; let's go," said Allon. With that Allon started down the road, with Jon following and speaking rather profoundly in a tone not unlike a mutter.

They had not traveled far when their path brought them to a creek. As they paused for a drink, Allon noticed something on the far bank, just off to the left, where the bank turned into a cliff. It was actually something on top of the cliff that caught his eye. "See that tree? It's the same as the others up there and yet different. It stands out from the rest, the same, yet different. It is the one that catches the attention amongst a forest of trees that do not. That is what you are to me, one of the Eadar, yet one that captures the attention.

"You are worried about walking to a 'different beat' from everyone else. I know not much about this; but I do know what it is about you that has earned my attention and my respect. You actually live what you believe. Not all in Eadar really do. You are bold enough to ask the tough questions, relentless in finding the answers and are then courageous enough to live your life according to the answers found. It is my uninformed, outsider's opinion that your 'drummer' knows his business quite well. You would do well to keep listening."

Jon stood silent for a while and stared up at that tree. He began to feel much better about the rhythms his drummer had been playing, about being himself. "Thank you, Allon. I needed to hear that."

"It is simply the truth...you're welcome."

Still gazing at that one tree, Jon added, "I never knew that's how you felt."

"Yes, well, don't let it go to your head."

"Never. Life is full of surprises, isn't it?" said Jon.

"Huh?" replied Allon.

"I always suspected it was there, but I never thought to see it," replied Jon.

Allon now turned his gaze to the tree, to see what Jon was looking at. "What are you talking about?" he asked. Still not seeing anything surprising atop the cliff.

"Tenderness, Allon, compassion. I have finally seen the softer side of the great Allon."

There was a slight pause. Jon was definitely his old self again. "Yes, well, if granny's gotten enough rest, we still have very far to go." So speaking Allon got underway, rather briskly. Jon followed once again, though this time, he was the one laughing and in a tone that was most unlike a mutter.

Travel safely, good friends. Travel safely.

OUT OF THE STORM

Tom sat quietly and watched the storm outside rage. He could not remember it ever having rained so hard. He would travel no further this day. While he was watching, lightning suddenly danced from ground to sky and back again while the howling wind toppled a tall tree. No he would travel no further this day. He settled back, grateful for the warmth of his fire; he might as well rest while he can. As he continued watching the violent side of nature, another storm came to mind, one from long ago. One so violent, the landscape of his life was forever changed.

Tom had lived in the village of Elberon of clan Eller. It was a small village belonging to the smallest of all the Eadarian clans. It had been a good home, and he loved it still. Yet the storm he now remembered had ripped it all away and left him branded Jarr-Dann—one banished for the sake of the king.

Imposing the sentence of Jarr-Dann was the most severe punishment a noble lord could impose. It had been devised solely as a punishment for the darkest of criminals, those who intentionally plotted against the king. It was a complete and everlasting banishment from king and clan. Never could the Jarr-Dann return home, under pain of death. When a noble lord inflicted this punishment, he would declare to the assembly, "I hereby declare that this never-ending exile is hereby imposed for the sake of the king and this, his country..."

"For the sake of the king..." Tom sighed aloud, as he reached over and stirred the coals of his fire. He watched the flames blaze anew and shook his head at the irony of his being so branded. Tom and others like him had been exiled for taking a stand on behalf of the king, not against him. "Banished for the sake of the king..." He repeated as he added more fuel to the fire; then he leaned back and closed his eyes against the memory that now washed over him like a flood.

The answer as to how a stand taken on behalf of the king could lead to such condemnation lies in whom these stands were actually against. They were always taken against a member of the nobility, but one who had become less noble and more self-serving, one whose focus had shifted from leading and protecting to controlling and manipulation.

The lord Tom had taken a stand against was Sir Woller, the ruling lord of clan Eller. It was thought that Woller's fall from true nobility began when emissaries of the Dark Lord Brokine, the enemy who hates forever, first gained access to his court. It was rumored that they were sent to broker peace with the fierce, if very small, clan Eller. Tom turned his gaze to the fallen tree outside and said aloud, "Rumors...shifting shadows whose origins are elusive and whose terminations are difficult to achieve." Regardless of why, the emissaries did arrive. With alarming rapidity, they went from being mere messengers of Brokine to being advisors on international diplomacy. Eventually they became Woller's most trusted advisors on every matter and rarely did they leave his side.

In harmony with this progression, Woller became ill at ease with anything that could arouse Brokine's disapproval. For as his new advisors would ask, "How can you expect to maintain your new exalted position of peacemaker if you continue to do things which arouse the displeasure of the great Brokine?" So it came to be that the banners of the king were taken from the castle walls. The statue celebrating the founding of their nation was removed from the courtyard. In due time, the people were even forbidden from speaking their king's name in public. These signs of hope, pride, and identity for the Eadarian people were now sources of embarrassment to

Woller. Merely because his new "friends" felt they were signs of unreasoning arrogance. Though for his part, Brokine never removed his banners, or anything honoring himself in a return display of good will.

The skies of Tom's life began to darken when he publicly questioned these changes. At first he only asked general questions such as: "Why is not peace being brokered with the king?" "Can one small clan mediate peace for this entire nation?" "What should we care what outsiders think of our nation and king?" These questions were bothersome but easily diverted since they required no great proofs in order to be answered. But the skies went from dark to stormy, and the storm intensified quickly when he began to ask specific questions that were tied directly to Woller and which demanded authentic evidence in the answering. "Sir Woller, where are the king's proclamations that you have received saying that these changes should be so? Show us, oh noble one, that we may believe," or again, "Sir Woller, we've taken down our banners, removed our statues; what has your new friend done to show his lack of arrogance, his commitment to peace?" Questions such as these did not sit well with Woller or with his new advisors. Something had to be done. Tom was making too much sense. With more and more of his clansmen beginning to call for a stop to all these changes, it was decided: Tom had to be silenced.

"But how?" asked Woller. "He is too well liked for any direct action. That would only raise the resistance in others."

"Agreed," said the advisors. "This needs to be done subtly. We have some experience in such matters and know the best way to accomplish this."

"How?" asked Woller.

"Softly spread rumors."

"Rumors?" replied the incredulous Woller, who was imagining something more intricate, more sophisticated, and demanding.

"Yes, rumors," came the reply. "For it matters not where they come from nor even if they are true. It only matters that they take hold. Trust us. Rumors have silenced more good men than swords ever could. Just send men out to the busy, crowded places in town. Have them whisper that they have heard, from a trusted and well-placed friend, that the king did approve our changes. Then in other places have it whispered that they have heard that this Tom is a troublemaker. That his outcries are bound to start unnecessary trouble."

"What trouble?" asked Woller.

"Weren't you listening?" asked his advisors. "Rumors need not be true. They only have to take hold, and the best rumors are those with the threat of personal pain for the listeners. These have been our greatest tools in the changing of public opinion."

"Rumors? And I have to do nothing else?" asked the very intellectual Woller.

"That's right. Just let them work and keep new ones flowing."

Tom shifted his gaze from the fire back to the tempest outside. It was beginning to weaken. It was a good thing they didn't last forever. Rumors, once started, were almost impossible to dispel. It took good men and women standing together, for when good folks stood together much could be accomplished. But when they did not, small-mindedness would abound. Small-mindedness was a mighty weapon in the decimation of a good man. As Tom stirred the coals of his fire, he came to realize that rumors were like smoldering coals, which, when gently fanned, could burst forth into flame. It could be a slow progression, but it was a sure one.

The first rumors were that Tom was naïve, ignorant, and a self-serving troublemaker. One who was not to be listened to. As he continued to voice opposition to Woller's changes, newer, darker, and more revealing rumors began to surface. Tom's credibility and reputation began to crumble. Fewer and fewer folks would speak openly with Tom. Then even fewer would meet with him in private. There were dark penetrating stares by those who thought he was unaware. And then, most painful of all, his close friends began to avoid him. They accused him of not caring about them, or about the bad reflection that he now cast their way. They said, "It's bad enough that you have brought yourself down, but leave us out of it!"

Tom's storm turned its blackest when he, compelled by love for his king and this, his country, began to protest just how costly this peace with Brokine had been. At a clan meeting Tom went so far as to say that this peace was truly not peace but a subversive war that Brokine was now winning. He said, "Just look at all we have lost of ourselves and look at how much ground Brokine has gained. It is no longer our king's rule that guides but Brokine's rules that govern us; and this without him having to spend so much as one arrow, not one single sword stroke."

Now it was that Woller got to witness the true power of rumors. From somewhere in the back of the room, the whispers came. Whispers that first turned into muttering, then matured into cries, and built into shouts of how treasonous it was to make such a statement. Then there was a very loud demand to know how one could take such direct opposition to the leadership appointed by the king. Was not opposition to his leaders the same as direct opposition to the king himself? This brought a chorus for cheers. Tom was stunned into silence; while he had not expected to win friends speaking the truth, he had not expected this. Nor was it long before such shouted statements led to calls for Tom's expulsion, calls for a purging of this trouble from their midst. Tom was arrested, tried, and banished by noon the next day. It all happened so fast, so fast. The might of any storm is in its chaos; this one was overwhelming. His life was torn apart.

But that was years ago, strange he should remember it now. As Tom continued to ponder this, he became aware of a ray of light that had spread across the floor in front of him. The outside storm had passed. He walked to the entrance of his shelter and gazed out. Evidence of the storm's passage was abundant; trees toppled, branches strewn about, and water stood everywhere. Yet for all that, there was now a crispness, a cleanness in the air that did not exist prior to the storm. Everything was fresher, more vibrant than before. He lowered his head, and a grin slowly spread across his face. Just as the king had said, "Nature imitates life." When his storm had finally passed, even with all the damage it made to the landscape of his life, he became more alive, more self-possessed, and more vitally trusting of his king than ever he was before. Perhaps these storms were not truly bad things after all. He stepped out from his shelter and noticed that the birds had already begun to sing. Perhaps he would travel a little farther this day after all. Yes, perhaps he would.

ABOUT THE AUTHOR

I am a storyteller by passion.

Over the past twenty years I've been telling stories when and as I could. I have told on college campuses, in coffee houses, at county festivals, to friends as we walk down the street, and to anyone interested in listening. In addition to this, I have been a volunteer reader for the Nashville Talking Library for over three years (this is a service for the visually impaired where books are recorded for future listening).

Over the past fifteen or so years, I have been writing my own stories. As I love all the noble aspects of the human experience, it is about these that I write and tell. Aspects such as: dedication to something or someone greater than oneself, respect, loyalty, laughter, tenacity, hope, and strength of character just to list a few. I am so passionate about this side of real life, that I only want to portray them in stories that are full of integrity, stories that are well crafted, and ones that are worth a second, third, and even a one hundredth read.

Even though these characters and stories are all fictional, there are some similarities to real life. For instance in these stories you will find good men and women. But just as in real life, they are only good men and women. Don't be so libelous as to call them perfect; once a person is so labeled it is too easy to tear them apart for being what they are, human. Good people do have strengths and they do have weaknesses. But good people do not allow their weakness to rule, nor do they allow these to keep them down once they've stumbled. In accepting good folks for what they are, we can then draw strength for the fact that we are not alone, that we are part of a great community of good men and women. There is great comfort and strength in knowing that one is not alone. So thinks this good man.

Enjoy.

You can contact Charles
at the Eadarian website
www.eadarian.com.